Vinnie Wiggins
and the
Tree Witch

Other books by Julia Jarman

Pillywiggins
and the
Tree Witch

JULIA JARMAN

Illustrated by Alex Bitskoff

Andersen Press • London

First published in 2011 by
Andersen Press Limited
20 Vauxhall Bridge Road
London SW1V 2SA
www.andersenpress.co.uk
Reprinted 2011, 2012

British Library Cataloguing in Publication Data available.

ISBN 978 1 84939 018 7

Printed and bound by CPI Group (UK) Ltd, Croydon,
CR0 4YY

To Mum and all my
family in The Deepings

With thanks to Arlene Brewin
for her exquisite Pillywiggins.

Chapter 1

There was a rabbit sitting in the fir tree.

The tree looked like a person. But then, trees often did if you were Natasha. She saw faces in all sorts of things, like on the pink chest of drawers in her bedroom or in the pattern on her wallpaper.

She was sitting in bed, looking out of the window. The view was still new to her as she had only just moved to the countryside. She lived at 7 Riverside Road, The Deepings and she liked her new address. Deepings made her think of water and stones dropping into it and ripples. There was a river at the end of the road.

The tree was a witch she decided. The rabbit was sitting on its arm. So how did the

rabbit get there? She wondered, and why hadn't it fallen off? It wasn't real, of course. Everyone knows that rabbits can't fly or climb. It must be a toy. So who put it there? The witch?

'It's just a tree,' she reminded herself as her mother looked round the door.

'Who are you talking to, Natasha?' Mrs Quillen was holding Charlie Baby.

'No one.'

'Tasha.' Her little brother reached out with both hands. 'Play.'

'Not this morning, Charlie.' Her mother was already heading downstairs. 'Natasha has to get up and get ready for school. Jonathan is up already.'

Jonathan was Natasha's older brother, and never stopped boasting about it. As if he could take the credit for being born first. He was probably downstairs hogging the computer right now.

The rest of the morning, in fact the rest of the day, was filled with ordinary things like getting dressed and having breakfast and going to school. Actually school didn't feel ordinary yet as Natasha didn't know anyone very well. She thought she was starting to make a friend called Lydia, but she wasn't sure.

When she got home, the rabbit was still sitting in the tree, but seemed to have slipped lower down the branch. It looked even more worried. And no wonder – the branches were swishing up and down and looked darker. The day was cloudy. It was early June but not at all summery.

School hadn't gone particularly well. Lydia hadn't been so friendly. Nor had the other girls. They couldn't pronounce her name they said, so they were going to call her Titch. Natasha didn't like being reminded she was rather small for her age.

Grumpily, she gazed out of her window. A rabbit in a tree. A tree like a witch. Those were the first signs she thought later, when she looked back. Natasha knew from the start there was something different about The Deepings.

Even before she met Pillywiggins.

Chapter 2

Natasha would probably never have met Pillywiggins if she hadn't stopped to talk to a boy on the way to school. He had longish brown hair and he was skimming stones from the riverbank.

'Good one,' she called out, when one of them bounced five times.

He looked up, but then picked up another stone and turned away, so she set off again. He obviously didn't want to talk and she didn't want to be late for school.

The river ran alongside the road on her right. She had to cross an old stone bridge to get to the High Street on the other side. The bridge had triangle-shaped inlets, three each side, hanging over the water, and she stopped in the middle one for traffic to pass. Natasha spotted Lydia on the High Street, walking with some other girls.

'Hi, Titch!' Lydia and the other girls waited.

When they reached the classroom, she saw the boy from the riverbank. He was sitting at a table with some other boys, but seemed separate from them somehow. None of them were talking to him. When Miss Rogers called the register, Natasha learned his name was Jamie.

Natasha was at a table of five with Lydia, a girl called Tanya and two boys. Miss Rogers had put her there on her first day.

Later, when they went outside for PE and had to get in sixes for a beanbag race, Lydia said, 'Now, who shall we have for our sixth person?'

'He's good at throwing.' Natasha pointed to Jamie.

But the other two girls shook their heads slowly from side to side. Lydia wrinkled her nose.

But Natasha noticed that the group he was in won. Lydia told her later that he was unpopular because he wouldn't play in the Saturday League, even though he was the best footballer in the class.

When he passed Natasha in the dinner queue she thought he looked a bit scruffy. He was coming back from the serving hatch with his tray and she saw that the cuffs of his sweatshirt were frayed. He caught her eye briefly and she had the feeling that he wanted to say something.

But he didn't.

Later though, at home time, she was at the pegs collecting her bag when suddenly he was by her side, muttering something in her ear.

Then he was gone.

'What did he say?' Lydia shuddered.

Tanya held her nose.

Natasha shrugged and shook her head. 'I've no idea.'

But she had. She knew exactly what he'd said.

Chapter 3

'Got something to show you. Meet me at the other side of the bridge.' That's what he'd said.

Should she? None of the other kids would. What could he want to show her? Was it a trick?

When she got out of school she couldn't see him. She still couldn't as she made her way towards the High Street with Lydia and her friends, or when they stopped to chat in front of The Bell. She kept her eye on the other side of the street, but not so the others would notice.

When they'd all gone in different directions, she crossed the bridge warily, fearing that he might jump out of one of the triangular inlets.

But he didn't. He was standing in front of a big old house with a FOR SALE board in the garden. She made out the words Fairfax House engraved on the gatepost.

'Hi,' said Natasha awkwardly.

'Fairyfax, that's what this house used to be called.' Jamie looked at her searchingly, gauging her reaction.

She was surprised a boy could say 'fairy' without sneering, but didn't comment.

'Fairies used to play in the garden,' he said quietly. 'You want to see it, don't you? I'll show you a short cut to your house.'

'How?' The gates were locked.

Fairfax House looked deserted. A red-leaved plant covered the walls and some of the windows. The grass in front hadn't been cut for ages.

'Come on.' He squeezed through a gap in the railings and set off up the drive.

'Are we allowed?' she asked, as he pushed open a rusty side gate.

She couldn't see a path – it was like a jungle – but he seemed to know where he was going. Sometimes he held back a thorny branch for her, but mostly he forged through the undergrowth. Trees towered overhead. Bees buzzed from the insides of flowers. She recognised roses and hollyhocks and nettles.

'Ouch!'

'Try this.' He handed her a rough leaf. 'It's a dock leaf. Spit on it and rub it on the sting.'

It worked.

She looked around her and thought of Sleeping Beauty and the forest that had grown for a hundred years, but Jamie was no prince. Her mum would say he was 'a bit rough'. Natasha didn't know what she thought, but there was a wildness to him, as though he was more at home in the woods than in the classroom.

'I can't be late home,' she said, when she caught up with him.

They were standing under a fir tree with wide-spreading branches. 'You won't be. See. I told you it was a short cut. Your garden used to be part of the Fairfax estate.' He pointed at a row of houses and she realised that one of them was hers. In fact she was looking up at her bedroom. Her fairy-mobile was hanging in the window and some of her fairy dolls were on the sill. The tree they were standing under was the one she could see when she was sitting up in bed.

It cast a cold shadow.

She was wondering if the rabbit was still there when Jamie dived off again. When she caught up with him he was standing in front of a statue, though she could only see it when he trampled down the grass.

'Pillywiggins.' He pointed at the statue. 'That's her name. She's a fairy.'

Cross-legged, sitting on a mushroom, the statue looked more like a gnome or pixie than a fairy, but Natasha decided to look at it again later. She'd suddenly remembered that her mum had said she'd meet her out of school. 'I've got to go. How do I get into my garden?'

'Come on. We can go through your fence.' He held back some loose slats while she climbed through.

'Don't go back there alone, right?' he said, when they were both through. Then he was off by the side of her house.

Chapter 4

Her mum was at the front door with Charlie in his buggy.

'Who was that boy, Natasha? And where have you been?' Mrs Quillen was cross. 'We came to meet you, didn't we, Charlie? I'm sure I told you.'

'Sorry. I forgot.'

Charlie wasn't cross. His round face creased in smiles as soon as he saw Natasha, and she started to get him out of the buggy.

'Careful, Natasha. Don't drop him.' Her mum could be so annoying.

Natasha played with Charlie for about an hour, then changed into jeans and went outside.

Don't go back there alone. Who did that boy think he was?

Checking her mum wasn't at the kitchen window, Natasha climbed through the hole in the fence. Now where was the statue? She had to stand on tiptoe to see the top of its head, but she kept low as she made her way towards it. Jonathan might be spying from his bedroom window.

As Natasha parted the stems to make a path, she felt like a giant spying on a secret world. A small, striped snail clung to a swaying blade of grass. A bumblebee crawled into a foxglove.

But another giant towered over her, casting a dark shadow. Now the fir tree definitely looked like a witch in a long, black cloak, swishing her arms and hissing: 'Stay away. Stay away.'

That's what it sounded like to Natasha.

'Shan't,' she said defiantly, standing up and forgetting she was trying to stay hidden. *Where was the statue? It ought to be around here.*

As she searched, the swishing branches got louder. 'Stay away. Stay away.'

But Natasha took no notice. She spotted the ears and found the statue.

Not a garden gnome, was her first thought. The statue was old – the stone green and brown and crusty with lichen – but it wasn't a little old man with a beard.

'Stay away. Stay away.'

Now goose pimples prickled her arms as a wind got up, shaking the tree's branches. But only the fir tree, she noticed. Weird.

'Shut up.' She was glad no one could hear her talking to a tree.

She turned back to the statue. It was a girl. Her oval face was a girl's. Her heavy-lidded eyes were a girl's. Her turned-up mouth was a girl's. She sat like a girl, on a mushroom, with her long legs crossed at the ankles. But she was dressed like a boy, well, an elf or pixie. Her short tunic had a zigzag hemline and Natasha could imagine her dancing on her pointed feet.

'But you're not human, not with those ears.'

'No, she's Pillywiggins.'

'Who...?' Natasha turned and there was Jamie.

She hadn't heard him approach and felt a bit stupid.

'A fairy,' he went on. 'I told you the old name for this place was Fairyfax.'

'But she hasn't got wings.'

'She did, but Tree Witch stole them and turned her into a statue.'

'Tree Witch? You're joking.'

But he didn't even smile. 'Don't tell me you don't know. You do. I saw it in your face the first time we met. That tree, the yew, it can change its shape. It used to be Green Lady, but now it's Tree Witch. If anything crosses her, she puts a spell on it. How do you think that rabbit got up there? It is real you know.'

The rabbit was still there – she checked – though Tree Witch, no the tree, was shaking its branches wildly. 'Stay away. Stay away.'

'We'd better be careful,' he went on. 'You don't have to do a lot to annoy her if she's in a bad mood, which she definitely is right now.'

'What did . . . er, Pillywiggins do?'

'Nothing. It wasn't Pillywiggins's fault. The fairies stole Green Lady's baby, so she turned into Tree Witch because she was so angry.

Now she's at war with the whole of the fairy kingdom. She just wanted a hostage. Revenge really. She managed to catch Pillywiggins when she was on the surface and put a curse on her. Pillywiggins is a bit of a loner,' he added.

Like you, thought Natasha, *and I can see why.*

'Most fairies are troopers,' he went on. 'They flit around in troops and look more like the fairies in your bedroom. But they aren't sweet little things like most girls think they are. Some of them don't care how much harm they do. Pillywiggins is different. She's not a trooper and it's not fair that Tree Witch put a curse on her.'

'Curse?' Natasha was even more confused.

'The spell that turned her into a statue.' He jerked his head up at the tree. 'Listen to her. She's in a really bad mood.'

'Stay away! Stay away!' howled Tree Witch.

'She's in a rage because it's a full moon tonight and that's when Pillywiggins comes alive for an hour. A full moon can lift a curse. You could see her – Pillywiggins I mean – if you stayed awake tonight.'

'I'll do that then.' She laughed, just in case he was joking, but he looked serious. Weird. And – weirder – some of what he said rang true.

There was something spooky about that tree.

Thinking about Tree Witch kept Natasha awake that night. It was the time of year when it takes ages to go dark. She lay tossing and turning, watching the sky turn from blue to pink and purple. For a while the horizon blazed pink, orange and gold, and the tree, silhouetted against it, looked even more like a witch.

A black-cloaked witch dancing in front of a fire.

Her arms swayed and her long fingers twitched. Then, at last, the sky deepened to a velvety blue-black and the moon appeared, at first just a pale, papery circle. Then it started to glow, as if someone was filling it with silver.

Natasha gave up trying to go to sleep. She went to the window and looked out at the garden flooded with silvery moonlight. Then she saw something moving. The statue? Or was it moonlight playing on the top of the statue's head? No. It really had moved. Yes, there it was again.

Natasha remembered Jamie's words: 'It's a full moon tonight and that's when Pillywiggins comes alive.'

Chapter 5

Pillywiggins could feel the moonbeams playing on her hard surface. She could feel herself softening. Feel life tingling through her. She wiggled her ears. She wriggled her toes. Even better.

But Tree Witch loomed overhead, hissing angrily:

*'Struggle, struggle for all you're worth
Pillywiggins, you're stuck on earth.'*

No I'm not, thought Pillywiggins. She didn't waste her breath replying, instead she put all her effort into standing up. After a few wobbly tries she succeeded. She stood on top of the mushroom, feeling its velvety surface beneath her feet. She stretched and waved her arms.

And Tree Witch cackled:

> 'Struggle, struggle for all you're worth
> I've got your wings, so you'll stay on earth.'

For a while Pillywiggins kept trying, waving her long arms hopefully and jumping high in the air. Could she take off? Could she fly without her wings? Just a short way? She only wanted to get to Natasha's house. Well, tonight she did. Later, if she could get her wings back...

Pillywiggins had been full of hope ever since she'd seen Natasha. The girl would help her, she felt sure. She had the power. Pillywiggins felt it when Natasha kneeled before her and looked into her eyes. She'd hoped and hoped Natasha would return that night, but she hadn't so Pillywiggins must go to her.

'Can't! Can't! Can't!' Tree Witch sounded as if her sides were splitting with laughter. But the moon was working her magic. Pillywiggins felt it pouring into her, not enough to fly perhaps, but enough to jump down and hurry to

Natasha's garden. Hurry she must, for she only had a short time to do what she needed to do.

Guided by a moonbeam, she made her way to the hole in the fence.

What now? Natasha had put back the broken slat, but there was a small gap, big enough for a fairy to squeeze through. *Made it!* Now she flitted across the mown grass, almost flying, till she was standing beneath Natasha's bedroom window.

'Help me!' Pillywiggins saw the girl leaning out. But could the girl see her? Could she hear her?

Chapter 6

'Help me!' A whisper came from below.

Natasha leaned further out and there she was, the fairy, on the patio. A single moonbeam highlighted her elfin features.

'Help me!' Pillywiggins's eyes, like glistening black berries, looked straight into Natasha's.

'How?' Natasha whispered. 'Tell me how.'

But there was no answer.

Natasha shivered. Suddenly a cold wind was blowing.

'Stay away. Stay away.' She could hear Tree Witch hissing and a cloud flew over the moon. Now she couldn't see Pillywiggins, so she spoke into the darkness.

'How? How can I help you? Tell me.'

The only answer was a cackle from Tree Witch, 'Can't! Can't! Can't!'

'How? Try and tell me how.' Natasha raised her voice, hoping the fairy was still there listening.

Still no answer, just a flash near the ground. Then a light like a laser zooming away from her straight through the fence.

Later, when the moon came out from behind the cloud, Natasha saw the top of the statue glimmering in the moonlight.

Pillywiggins was back on her mushroom. Stone again.

And Tree Witch was hissing, 'Stay away!'

Chapter 7

Pillywiggins was hurting.

The hardening hurt.

Ever since Tree Witch's hatred shot through her, wrenching her back to the garden, she'd felt an icy pain spreading through her. Now she was stone, but while her body became hard and motionless she carried on thinking and feeling. That was the witch's cruellest act.

Pillywiggins knew she looked like a statue, but she felt like a fairy.

Now she fought feelings of despair.

There will be another chance.

I did make contact with Natasha.

I was right about her.

Natasha is a good girl, a kind girl, a brave girl, just the sort of girl to challenge Tree

Witch's evil power. Pillywiggins was sure of it. She'd seen the tenderness in her eyes. Jamie had it too and he had tried when she asked him, but he couldn't find the fairy ring.

Natasha wants to help me, Pillywiggins comforted herself. And she won't give up!

I'll try to reach her tomorrow when the full moon frees me with her life-giving light.

Chapter 8

'Help me!'

The fairy's words were in Natasha's head when she woke up early the next morning. *I must talk to Jamie before school*, was her next thought.

She found him on the riverbank. 'I s-saw her,' she said hesitantly, still half expecting him to laugh.

But he didn't. He didn't even say 'who?' So she told him everything she'd seen and heard the night before.

'So, are you going to help?' His brown eyes looked serious.

'How can I?'

'Find out what she wants.'

'How?'

'Ask her. Try again tonight if you can, but you might have to wait till the next full moon.'

As they started to walk to school he said it all depended on whether the moon was waxing or waning. 'Sounds as if the curse wasn't completely lifted last night. You said she stayed on the ground, didn't you? That means she didn't have enough magic energy to climb. That might be because the moon wasn't completely full...'

'Or,' Natasha surprised herself with her next thought, 'it might be because Tree Witch was countering the moon's magic with her own.'

They were nearly at the bridge and Jamie said, 'You go ahead. You don't want the others to see you with me.'

She was about to say, 'I don't care,' though she still wasn't sure if that was true, when he said, 'Go on. I'm going to check on something.'

She didn't even have time to ask what before he darted into the driveway of Fairfax House. She didn't see him again till he came into the classroom, five minutes after the bell had gone, and he kept out of her way for the rest of the day.

That didn't stop Tanya from making annoying remarks. 'Not talking to your boyfriend today, Titch? Had a tiff have you?'

Lydia was no better and Natasha was too tired to think of a cutting reply. Besides, she had other things on her mind, like how did Jamie know all this stuff? Why wasn't he helping Pillywiggins? She made up her mind to ask him after school, but when the last bell went he disappeared fast. And he wasn't waiting on the other side of the bridge.

By the end of the day she was even more tired and didn't mind when her mum sent her to bed early. The only problem was trying to stay awake till Pillywiggins came. *If* she came. Natasha propped herself up on her pillows but her eyes kept closing, so she set an alarm for just before midnight.

When it went off it was dark and the moon, round and white, shone into her bedroom.

Tap tap tap. A sound drew her back to the window. There was a bright light bobbing up and down.

'Help!' The fairy was tapping the glass.

Natasha was out of bed in a second. 'Stand back.'

Carefully she opened the window and held out her hand. And the fairy stepped onto it! So this was Pillywiggins. She had never seen anything so strange and beautiful.

'I climbed,' she gasped as she sat in the palm of Natasha's hand, dangling her long legs over the edge. 'The honeysuckle helped. Now, listen please. I need your help. There are three things—'

'Three!'

'One, find my wings. Two, find the portal to Fairy Land . . . That's the fairy ring. It seems to have disappeared, and it's the only way back to Fairy Land. Three, help me . . .'

But before she could finish, a sound like splitting wood rent the darkness.

'Can't! Can't! Can't!' screamed Tree Witch.

But Pillywiggins persisted. '. . . Help me find Green Baby, Tree Witch's child . . .'

'Caaa-n't!' As another cry from Tree Witch filled her ears, Natasha tried to concentrate.

'Tree Witch says the fairy ring has gone for ever, and so I must remain a statue for ever, but...' Pillywiggins's voice was faint now. 'It is still here. It must be *here*. Fairy rings are never completely destroyed. Please, take me...to it...so I can bring Green Baby back and make everything...the rabbit, everything, right again.'

Then she was gone.

It was the same as last time, except that Natasha felt the icy shock as the fairy streaked from her hand, back to the garden of Fairfax House.

Chapter 9

'What exactly did she say?' asked Jamie, glancing over Natasha's shoulder. They were in the writing corner of the classroom.

'She said, "The fairy ring is still here. Here." She said that twice.'

'I'll think about it,' said Jamie. 'You'd better go and sit down.'

After school he was waiting for her on the other side of the bridge. 'Thought we could go and ask my gran.'

'Why?'

'She knows about these things. She's a Romany and when she travelled here as a girl she saw the fairies . . . Let's go and see her.'

'Now?' Natasha knew she ought to go straight home.

'As soon as possible.'

'Where does your gran live?'

'By Low Lock, just outside the village. It won't take long. When she saw the fairies your road wasn't even built so I reckon she'll know where the fairy ring used to be.'

A Romany! Natasha was a bit disappointed when they arrived at a cottage by the river. She'd hoped for a colourful caravan and a camp fire, not a kitchen.

The old lady was asleep in a rocking chair, her face brown like a shrivelled old conker.

'Ninety next birthday,' said Jamie. 'She's a bit deaf but she's got all her marbles.'

'Marbles?' Natasha whispered.

'Brains,' said the old lady, opening her eyes, which were bright and brown like Jamie's. 'That's what he means. And I'm not so deaf as he thinks. Make me a cuppa, Jamie, and tell me what you've come for.'

Jamie explained why they'd come, but when he asked where the fairy ring was she said, 'What you want to know for? I told you to leave well alone.'

'Because Pillywiggins asked Natasha to take her to it.'

'The girl?' The old lady looked Natasha up and down. 'What she say then?'

Natasha told her what Pillywiggins had said.

'Don't need to ask me then. Use your own marbles,' said the old lady sipping her tea. 'She's told you, ain't she? Tell me again what she said. And listen to yourself this time.'

'Take me to the fairy ring,' said Natasha, remembering the fairy sitting in the palm of her hand. 'It is still here. Here. Fairy rings are never completely destroyed.'

'And where were you when she said it?' The old woman's voice was brusque.

'In my bedroom.'

'Well, she said "here," didn't she? So that's where it is, in your house. Where do you live?'

Natasha told her and the old woman gazed into the distance as if seeing something.

'Yes, that's where it always was, so that's where it'll always be.' She put down her cup and closed her eyes, then opened them suddenly. 'Would you know the ring if you saw it though?' When Natasha shook her head, the old woman explained that it was a ring of lush, dark grass, growing among the meadow grass. 'Well, it was when Riverside Road was part of the Fairyfax estate. With mushrooms, big white flat caps. Delicious.'

'It can't be upstairs in my house,' said Natasha as they walked home. She wasn't at all sure that the old woman had all her marbles.

'And what did your gran mean when she said, "I told you to leave well alone"?'

'I've asked her before,' said Jamie, reddening, 'and she said it was too dangerous to tell me.'

'Why did you ask her?'

'Because Pillywiggins asked me to help find the fairy ring, I looked but I couldn't find it anywhere.'

When Natasha got home she searched all the lower rooms in the house, looking for a sign, like a touch of green on the carpet, or even a damp patch. Nothing. And nothing out of the ordinary happened for the rest of the week.

But on Friday night she saw something amazing.

Chapter 10

Everyone else was asleep.

Natasha was creeping downstairs to get a drink when she saw it happening. It stopped her mid-step. Blades of bright-green grass were growing through the sitting-room carpet! A ring of bright-green grass was shooting up in the middle of the room. Then came the mushrooms. Creamy-white domes popped up, one, two, three...

Natasha counted under her breath till the circle was complete with nine mushrooms.

A fairy ring. She could hardly believe it, even when a fairy appeared in the middle of it.

'Phew! Made it.' The fairy's long hair floated like a golden halo. Her gauzy dress shimmered with all the colours of the rainbow.

'Out of the way!' Another fairy appeared, flame red, pushing the rainbow fairy aside.

Natasha realised that the portal must be in the middle of the circle. Was there some sort of opening? She wondered, when a strident whisper made her turn round.

'Natasha!' It was her mum at the top of the stairs. 'What are you doing?'

'Getting a drink.'

But when she looked into the sitting room again, on the way to the kitchen, all she could see was beige carpet. Grass, mushrooms and the two tiny fairies had gone. Vanished.

She looked at the clock in the kitchen.

It was five minutes past midnight.

Chapter 11

The next morning it was raining and Natasha's mum wouldn't let her go outside. So she couldn't tell Jamie or Pillywiggins what she'd seen. The only good thing was that it was a Saturday. Jonathan and Dad were going to a football match, so she could get on the computer.

She instantly googled fairy rings.

> A fairy ring, also known as fairy circle, elf circle or pixie ring is a naturally occurring ring arc of mushrooms. May grow up to ten metres in diameter. The spores of the fungus calvatia cyathiformis cause the grass to grow more abundantly.

'Ha!' Jonathan looked over her shoulder. He was waiting for Dad to get changed. 'Bet you thought fairies made them.'

Natasha sighed and read on.

> A great deal of folklore surrounds fairy rings. They are associated with good and bad luck. Some cultures believe a house built on a fairy circle will bring prosperity to its inhabitants.

'Because they bury their little pots of gold there,' said Jonathan. 'Why don't you go outside and start looking, little sis'?'

'Why don't you go to your football match?'

> Others think building on a fairy circle results in punishment. A farmer who built a barn over one was struck down senseless.

It was a bit worrying.

'Many cultures believe a fairy ring is a portal to Fairy Land ...' That's what Pillywiggins had said.

… Mortals should avoid them for
fairies take malicious pleasure in luring
them inside … mortals who do so may
die or find it impossible to leave … or
become invisible or come back much
older than when they went in …

She couldn't help turning round to look for
Charlie who'd been playing on the carpet a
moment ago – where the fairy ring had been!
'Charlie?'
Then she saw him in the kitchen. Phew!
She went to give him a hug and her mum said,
'It's stopped raining. Didn't you want to go
outside, Natasha?'
She headed straight for Fairfax Garden.

Chapter 12

'Sss . . . tay away! Sss . . . tay away!'

Tree Witch started hissing as soon as Natasha stepped through the hole in the fence. She rocked and swayed as if she was in the middle of a swirling storm, but the rest of the garden was eerily calm.

'Sss . . . tay away! Sss . . . tay away!'

Natasha stood up and looked straight at the witch.

'I'm trying to help you. You,' she said emphatically. 'I'm going to tell Pillywiggins I've found the portal to Fairy Land. Then we're going to get your baby back.'

That seemed to shut her up.

For a bit.

Natasha started to make her way towards

Pillywiggins. It was easier than the other times. There was a bit of a track now where she'd trampled down the undergrowth.

But soon the tree started hissing again, 'Sss...tay away! Sss...tay away!'

The closer Natasha got to Pillywiggins, the more wildly Tree Witch shook, and the louder she hissed, 'Sss...tay away! Sss...tay away!'

She rained pine needles on Natasha's bare arms and face.

'Ouch!' They hurt.

'Sss...tay away! Sss...tay away!'

'I'm going to help Pillywiggins get your baby back!' Natasha shouted back. 'We're going to get Green Baby for you!'

But her words made no difference.

'Sss...tay away!'

'Be reasonable!' cried Natasha. 'Give us a chance!'

But witches aren't reasonable.

Holding up her hands to shield herself from the needles slowed Natasha down quite a bit, but she did at last reach Pillywiggins. No, the statue of Pillywiggins, she reminded herself, as she stood in front of her. Not a

living creature. Not at the moment. So could she hear?

Natasha kneeled down in front of her.

'I've found the fairy ring. It's in my house. Now what do I do?'

Chapter 13

Pillywiggins could hear Natasha.

She heard her say, 'I've found the fairy ring.'

But she couldn't reply.

She heard her say, 'Come to my house tonight at midnight. I'll open a window for you.'

But she couldn't say, 'I can't, not tonight. The moon is waning.' She tried to speak but the words stayed inside – straining to get out.

All she could do was will Natasha to keep trying to help her, and ignore Tree Witch's warnings.

Pillywiggins felt cold as the witch swished her branch arms angrily.

'You! You!'

Natasha didn't understand the witch. 'I know you're a yew,' she shouted. 'Jamie told me.'

'You! You! You!' The witch pointed her arms at Natasha, and Pillywiggins caught on. The witch wasn't saying, 'Yew!' She was saying, 'You'.

Now the brave girl was transfixed, staring up at the witch, and no wonder. Never before had the tree looked so much like a witch. She *was* a witch, a towering, spiky green witch. And never before had she sounded so much like a witch.

'The fairy stays.' She cackled clearly. '*She* won't come back to me if she goes to Fairy Land. *You* must go!'

Pillywiggins strained every atom to say, 'I would. I would come back with Green Baby,' but nothing came out. And now the witch was on the move. The horrible creature was whirling round. She was moving forward. Oh no! She had uprooted herself. Feet like gnarled roots were advancing towards Natasha.

'You,' she shrieked again, 'you must go and get my baby or...'

Pillywiggins trembled or would have if she could. She feared for Natasha. What was the witch threatening to do? What horrible punishment would she devise?

'. . . I'll get yours,' hissed the witch.

What did she mean? Pillywiggins didn't understand. The girl hadn't got a baby. She was too young. She went over the words in her head but they didn't make sense. Then she heard the witch screech, 'I'll turn him into a beetle!'

For several minutes the girl was speechless. Then she stammered, 'W-what? Who? You don't mean Charlie?'

'Watch!'

The witch pointed at a bird perched on a branch, a robin, its breast pale because it was summer.

Robin red, robin red!
Turn into a piece of bread!'

As light flashed from the witch's pointed finger, brown turned white as the bird turned into a piece of bread.

'Caw! Caw!' High in the sky, a crow spotted a tasty morsel and swooped down. 'Caw!' It flew off with the bread in its beak.

Pillywiggins saw Natasha freeze.

'See! See!' The witch was ecstatic.

'B–but you wouldn't do that to Charlie?' The girl was shivering.

'Fetch my baby. Ssss…oon!'

Pillywiggins felt an icy draught whirling round her.

'Or I'll get yours,' repeated the witch. 'I'll turn your brother into a beetle!'

Longing to help, Pillywiggins watched as Natasha staggered back to the hole in the fence.

Chapter 14

Natasha was still trembling as she entered the kitchen.

'Darling, what happened?' said her mum. 'You look as if you've seen a ghost.'

'A witch actually.'

Her mum laughed and hugged her. 'You and your imagination.'

'Where's Charlie?' Natasha wanted to cuddle him close.

'In the sitting room.'

He was on the carpet where the fairy circle had been.

'Come here, Charlie, sit by me.' She patted the sofa, but he wanted her to get on the floor with him. He was playing with a red post box with holes of different shapes.

'Help me, Tasha.' He was trying to post a yellow triangle through a square hole.

'I will, Charlie, I will.' If only it were as easy as matching shapes to holes.

Would the fairy circle appear again?

Dare she enter it and fetch Green Baby?

Charlie handed her the triangle and she knew she had to, when she saw his little finger.

The nail was black and shiny – like a beetle's back. Tree Witch had begun.

Chapter 15

When she told Jamie about Charlie's finger he went pale.

'We've got to do something. Now. Let's tell Tree Witch we'll try at the next full moon.'

'But that's a month away! Will that be soon enough?'

The garden was still and quiet when they looked at it through the gate. The buzz of a bumblebee was the only sound. That changed when they went in.

'Sssstay away,' hissed the witch. 'Sssstay away.'

The closer they got the more agitated the witch became. Crows flew from her branches in a bomb burst of black feathers.

'Sssstay away. Sssstay away
Unless you've come here to obey!'

'S-stop, Jamie.' She went to clutch his arm, but he'd gone.

He was ahead of her. She hurried after him, trampling grass and pushing back brambles till she reached him, standing in the tree's shadow.

'Tell Tree Witch.' Jamie grabbed Natasha's arm. 'Tell her you'll try at the next full moon.'

'I . . .' Natasha looked up at the horrible witchy face but she couldn't get the words out.

'T'night!' The witch mouth opened and closed showing black jagged teeth.

'But . . .'

'T'night!' Witch teeth gnashed. There was no mistaking what she was saying. 'Tonight! You, you, *you*, Natasha . . .'

Then silence. Even the bees had stopped buzzing. It was as if the whole garden was cowering under her gaze.

Chapter 16

As they left, the gate clanged shut like a tolling bell.

Jamie said he had to go shopping for his mother. It was the first time he'd mentioned her.

Natasha said, 'I'll come too.' She didn't want to be alone.

'Are you sure? What if we meet the girls from school?'

She shrugged. 'Compared to Tree Witch . . .'

On the way he said his mum was disabled, so he had to help her a lot. She couldn't walk. That's why he couldn't play in the Saturday League. 'And I think that's why Gran wouldn't help me find the ring and go to fetch Green Baby. She wouldn't let me take the risk of not coming back. Who would look after my mum?'

'But what if I don't come back,' Natasha couldn't help screaming.

'You must think I'm a coward,' he said. 'But I'll ask Gran if there's anything you can do to improve your chances of getting back.'

She told him he wasn't a coward, his gran was right. 'I think you're amazing to look after your mum.'

He was quiet then – till they got to The Bell on the way back, when he pointed to a poster on the pub wall.

Midsummer's Eve Disco
Saturday 23rd June.
Tickets £10

Someone had written SOLD OUT across it.

'So? You didn't want to go, did you?'

'No, but look what it says. Midsummer's Eve. Tonight. So the circle might be there – as it's a special night – even if there isn't a full moon. You should try at midnight tonight.'

'But will Pillywiggins be alive? I want to ask her where Green Baby is before I go.'

If I go, she wanted to add. But she knew she had to, as soon as she got home and saw Charlie's hand.

Another of his nails was shiny black.

Chapter 17

Mrs Quillen noticed Charlie's black nails when he was in the bath.

'What happened? Did you hit yourself with your hammer?'

Charlie loved his hammer and peg set, even though he sometimes bashed his fingers. Natasha watched as he splashed his hand in the water.

She had to do something. Tonight. But would the fairy ring be there?

Midsummer's Eve felt like the longest day of the year. The evening seemed to go on forever, especially when Natasha was alone in bed. The sky outside her window stayed bright blue and the dire warnings about fairy rings went round and round in her head.

'Mortals may become invisible.
Mortals may find it impossible to leave
or even die.'

She thought about the task ahead.

How could she find Green Baby without Pillywiggins to help? Where was he hidden? She wondered if any of her books could tell her. Was there a map of Fairy Land in any of them? Was there anything about fairies stealing babies? She flicked through one then another. There were no maps, but in one book it did say some trickster fairies stole human babies. She looked at her fairy collection. None of them looked like Pillywiggins. They were mostly pink and they all had wings.

Wings! Suddenly Pillywiggins's words were in her head. 'One, find my wings.' She had forgotten there were three tasks.

She rushed to the window and opened it wide.

'Pillywiggins!' she called softly at first, hoping her mum wouldn't hear her. When music and voices floated up from the TV below she called louder, 'Pillywiggins, I'm going to try and make you some wings!'

There was no response and she couldn't even see the statue. The grass had grown high in the warm summer weather.

'Pillywiggins, please help me find Green Baby!'

The only response was a hissing sound.

Tree Witch was stirring.

Chapter 10

Pillywiggins heard Natasha and longed to help her. She wanted to go to Fairy Land, if she could. If she could come to life, if she could outwit Tree Witch and reach the fairy ring, then she'd bring Green Baby back, she really would.

But I can't go, not without wings, and not till the next full moon unless, unless . . .

She felt a tingling in her toes. It was the same feeling she had when she was coming to life. Something magical was happening.

She could see it. Sense it. Something was breathing extra life into the plants around her. The blush pink of the roses was deepening. The creamy yellow of the honeysuckle was thickening. Leaves were glossier. Stems were

springier. And it wasn't just plants that seemed more alive. The buzzing of bees was so loud it was making the air vibrate.

'Mmmm...Midsummer's Eve.'

Was that what they were saying? Something in Pillywiggins quickened. She was coming alive.

'Mmmm...Mmmmmidsummer's Eve.'

Just a couple of days after the longest day of the year. That's why it seemed as if night would never come. But it will, it will...she longed for it to come and as an owl swooped low, blue sky turned grey.

A rabbit hopped into view and spoke. 'Save my brother, Pillywiggins.'

She wanted to say, 'I will if I can,' but couldn't speak.

The sky grew darker.

'Wish for some wings,' said the rabbit. 'It is Midsummer's Eve! Lizards grow new tails, so why can't you grow new wings?'

Pillywiggins concentrated hard and wished.

> *I wish for wings*
> *To make me fly.*
> *To help Natasha*
> *Who must not die.*

But nothing happened. She wished again. Still nothing.

Then she heard something creeping through the undergrowth.

Chapter 19

It was Natasha.

She had been busy, but she still had work to do – quietly. She didn't want Tree Witch to see or hear her.

'I've made you some wings. Well, I took them off one of my fairies. Just hope this glue will work.'

She had to be quick. Any moment now her mum or dad or even Jonathan might look in her room and see she had gone. They'd all been in bed when she crept out of the house but she wasn't sure if they were asleep. It had been half-past eleven by her bedside clock.

She had taken the wings off the largest fairy in her collection. They were made of gauzy green silk. She'd had to undo lots of tiny stitches but couldn't sew them onto Pilly-wiggins, not onto stone. Luckily the glue stuck, quite quickly!

'I've got to get back now,' Natasha whispered, willing the fairy to come to life.

If only Pillywiggins could talk to her, but she stayed as a statue.

'Come to my house as soon as you can, if you come to life. I'll leave the kitchen window open. I just want to know where to look for Green Baby, do you know?'

No answer, and she couldn't wait any longer.

As she crept back into the house the church clock started chiming.

'One, two, three...' she counted up to twelve.

Midnight! As the last note faded away she heard music coming from the sitting room. Lovely music made by flutes. It pulled her towards the sitting-room door and she knew the fairies were there when they began to sing.

'Step inside, step inside,
Step inside our fairy ring.
You will find, you will find...'

Her hand was on the door handle now, pressing it down and as it opened slowly she saw the fairies.

Chapter 20

The fairies were dancing, whirling and twirling among blades of emerald-green grass and velvety white mushrooms. In gauzy dresses with matching wings, pink, white and mauve, hundreds of tiny fairies danced on tiptoe. And round them more fairies rode bareback on tiny white unicorns with silver manes. Natasha had never seen such exquisite creatures. She had never seen such perfect footwork or heard such enchanting music. And now she saw the music makers, a band of green elves on spotty toadstools, holding flutes to their red lips.

'Step inside, step inside,
Step inside our fairy ring.
You will hear, you will hear
Magic bells go ting-ling-ling.'

As they sang some fairies shook silver bells and Natasha moved closer to hear them, as they intended. Their song had lured mortals to Fairy Land since time began.

> 'Step inside, step inside
> Put your foot on the green…'

She longed to hear the bells and ride on the back of a unicorn.

> 'We will take you
> We will take you
> To our dearest
> Fairy Queen.'

Suddenly she was very close, although she wasn't aware of moving. She towered over the fairies and longed to be tiny so she could enter Fairy Land.

And all the fairies were reaching out to her now. They had stopped dancing and she could feel their force. It was as if invisible ropes were tied to her ankles, pulling her towards the circle…

'We will take you
We will take you
To our dearest
Fairy Queen.'

The fairies sang on, pulling her closer and closer...

'Stop!' Foot on the edge of the circle she halted, and there was Jamie's frantic face pressed to the glass of the patio door.

'My gran says, walk round the circle nine times before you enter. Nine times or you'll never come back!'

Chapter 21

'I'm not doing what you say.' The voice coming out of Natasha's mouth was high and sweet like...like...a fairy's!

Now unicorns on hind legs formed an archway leading to the middle of the fairy ring.

'Just walk round it nine times,' Jamie implored.

'Go away,' said the silvery voice that wasn't hers, and something even stranger was happening. Natasha was collapsing into herself. She was folding up, shrinking. Suddenly all the little creatures: fairies, elves, unicorns, didn't seem so little. But the sofa at her side was as high as a cliff face, and the face looking through the patio window was a frantic giant's.

'Natasha, nine times, remember, nine times!'

But it was too late. A stronger force was drawing her forward. She was running under the unicorn archway, on tiptoe, almost floating, lured by the fairies' song.

'Come and join us,
Come and join us,
Come and meet our Fairy Queen.
Come and join us,
Come and join us,
You will never on earth be seen.'

Natasha didn't hear the last line, there was a rushing sound in her ears, like a waterfall. Nor did she see something tiny whizz past her for a new force was pulling her now, a whirling, swirling downward force. As the fairies danced in decreasing circles, faster and faster, they moved nearer to the vortex at its centre. And so did Natasha. Like water in a bath she felt herself surging forward,

spiralling downwards…
Down and round,
Down and round,
Down and round,
A silver whirlpool was carrying her to
realms unknown…

Chapter 22

Bump!

Natasha landed on something soft. She couldn't see what because she was surrounded by fairies. Some fluttered round her head. Others were pulling her away from fairies still sliding down. Tiny fingers tugged at her hands and pyjamas.

'Yan tan tethera, heave!'

They tickled and she couldn't help laughing – which blew the ones in front of her into the air. Though smaller, she was still bigger than they were.

Now elves were sliding down and unicorns on hooves slightly splayed. She just had time to notice the fairies forming a procession when they started to sing again.

'We will take you
We will take you
To our dearest
Fairy Queen…'

'But—' Natasha wanted to say something. She knew something was wrong, but a swarm of fairies was lifting her onto the back of a unicorn. When it started to move forwards, she had to concentrate on holding its mane. But there was something she had to do while she was here. She tried to remember what it was, but fairy song drowned her thoughts.

'You'll adore her,
You'll adore her,
Lovelier,
You've never seen.'

They were going along a winding road bordered by flowering trees. Now and then she caught a glimpse of a pretty cottage. She was passing through a fairy village, she realised. Some fairies were in their gardens. One was swinging on a gate and another was pushing a pram made from a walnut shell.

A pram with a baby in it. A baby! That was it. Green Baby! She had to find him. That was what she was here for. But now she had to hold on tighter to the silky mane, for the unicorn was climbing a steep hill. At the top she could see a palace with flags flying from turquoise turrets. A breeze filled her nose with the delicious scent of flowers, drowning her memories of Earth.

'Sit up straight. We're nearly there.' A fairy in bright yellow poked her.

'Taran ta taa!' Pixie musicians heralded their arrival as the unicorn trotted into a courtyard, paved with sparkling stones.

'Dismount,' said the bossy yellow fairy who had poked her, but while Natasha was wondering how to get off, more fairies lifted her onto the ground.

'Stand up straight!' That was Bossy Fairy again. 'Periwinkle, Pansy, lead the mortal to Her Majesty.'

Two mauve fairies took hold of Natasha's arms and led her up some stairs and through a door at the top. In front of them Bossy Fairy twirled her wand like a drum majorette.

'Try to move faster,' said Periwinkle. 'Her Majesty expects her subjects to pay homage at sunset. We won't all get through if you dawdle.'

'And Her Majesty has to dub you first,' said Pansy.

'D-dub?' Natasha didn't like the sound of that.

'Touch you with her magic wand, so you forget your mortal life and become one of her subjects. That's what you've come for, haven't you?'

'Do hurry up,' said Periwinkle as they reached the end of a corridor and double doors opened wide. At first Natasha was so dazzled by all the glittering chandeliers that she didn't see the golden thrones at the end of the room, or the two figures sitting on them.

'The Queen and the King.' Periwinkle squeezed Natasha's arm. 'You are doubly honoured.'

'But—'

'Silence in the presence of Their Majesties!' Bossy Fairy turned round to face Natasha.

'Walk to the stage, climb the steps and kneel.'

'What for?'

'The dubbing, so you can live with us for ever.' Bossy Fairy sighed. 'Fairies, you'd better take her.'

Now Periwinkle and Pansy took hold of Natasha's arms and airlifted her to the foot of the stage. Looking up, she saw the loveliest fairy she had ever seen and she longed to gaze at her forever. When the Fairy Queen beckoned, Natasha climbed the steps eagerly.

'Kneel,' said the Queen, raising her wand and Natasha sank to her knees.

Then suddenly she was whisked upwards, out of reach of the Fairy Queen's wand.

Chapter 23

Pillywiggins was invisible as she dropped from the sky. The girl needed her; there was no way she would get out of Fairy Land without her help.

Just in time she grabbed Natasha's hand and cast an invisibility spell on her. Natasha disappeared. Good. So far her rescue plan was working but there was a lot more to do. As she headed for the exit with Natasha in tow, Pillywiggins dropped a letter onto the Fairy Queen's lap. URGENT READ NOW it said on the envelope in bold letters.

Pillywiggins had been very busy since Natasha gave her new wings and Midsummer's-Eve magic had brought her to life. She had managed to leave the garden without being seen by Tree Witch.

She hadn't been quick enough to stop Natasha entering the fairy ring – the girl was too determined to go – but she had managed to enter soon after. Her plan was to rescue Green Baby, but first she must get Natasha back to the portal. Quickly. Before it closed. Natasha was in danger of staying here for ever.

There was uproar below. The King and Queen were on their feet, looking left and right. The letter was on the floor.

'She's escaped!' The Fairy Queen was furious. 'Find her! Quick! Before she makes her way to the portal. Mortals are not allowed back to Earth. Guards, why are you standing there?'

Some Red Goblin guards stuttered in reply, 'We can't see her, Your Majesty.'

'She b–became invisible,' said Bossy Fairy.

'Without my permission?' The Fairy Queen whirled round. 'How? Who would dare?'

Chapter 24

Natasha had no idea what was happening till she heard a voice cry, 'Duck!' as she zoomed under a doorway.

'Pillywiggins?' She thought she recognised her voice, but couldn't see who was towing her through the air at high speed.

'Prepare to land!'

Suddenly Natasha felt herself descending, then she landed behind a sparkling bush.

'Pillywiggins, are you really here?'

'Yes,' said the voice from behind her. 'Stand still while I fix these.'

'What?'

'Wings for you. I got them from a fairy doll in your bedroom and made them invisible.'

Natasha felt something pressing into her back.

'Zarabanda,
Stick, wings, stick
So we can fly,
Very quick.'

'Now flap your arms three times for take-off,' said Pillywiggins.

Natasha flapped and felt her feet leave the ground. She was flying all by herself! Amazing!

'Good,' said Pillywiggins. 'Now follow me.'

'But how...?' Natasha was about to say '...If I can't see you,' when she heard a high-pitched buzzing.

'It's the Red Goblins,' gasped Pillywiggins from in front of her. 'They're Fairy Land's top flying force. They're after you so fly for your mortal life.'

Soon Natasha could see the fairy village below – and when she looked back she could see the Red Goblins behind in a V-formation. 'Can they see us?'

'I think they've guessed that I'm taking you back to the portal,' said Pillywiggins.

'But you can't.' Natasha was thinking clearly now. 'Not without Green Baby. I've got to get him first. That's why I came.'

'Leave that to me.'

'I can't—' But before Natasha had time to explain that this was the only way to save Charlie, the buzz became an ear-piercing whine.

'Maybe you're right,' said Pillywiggins. 'Portal later. Must divert the goblins. Change direction and dive under their left wing. Kick your feet for added speed.'

Turning in midair, Natasha dived under the left flank of goblins. At first their whine got louder but gradually as she kicked her feet furiously, it lessened to a hum. Then after an age of kicking, silence – they'd given them the slip – and looking down she saw the terrain had changed. Cushions, that's what she thought of as she saw soft hummocks in different shades of green far below.

'Don't be deceived,' said Pillywiggins, who seemed to read her mind. 'That's the Dark Wood and that's where I think Green Baby is hidden. Look, there's a clearing. Start going down.'

'How?'

'Hold your arms in and stop kicking.'

Pleased to take a rest, Natasha felt herself floating down and thinking clearly. Find Green Baby. Take him to Tree Witch. Make Charlie safe. It was great to have help from Pillywiggins, but *she* had to return Green Baby to Tree Witch by herself.

Down.

Down.

They were nearly there, when – *ROAR!* A blast of hot air shot her skywards.

Chapter 25

'It's old Hot Breath,' said Pillywiggins, hovering beside her. 'He's the dragon who guards the wood. I should have guessed from the charred grass that he made the clearing. Don't worry, I can deal with him. It's the Brownies and Bugaboos we've got to look out for.'

'Brownies and Bugaboos?'

'Brownies look after the changelings; the stolen babies,' Pillywiggins went on. 'They look hideous. They haven't got mouths, so they shove food up their noses.'

'Ugh.' Fairy Land wasn't what Natasha had expected. Well, this part wasn't.

'Bugaboos are the guards; they rely on their stench to keep intruders away,' said Pillywiggins.

'But where is Green Baby?' asked Natasha, determined to focus on the task.

'Down there in the Dark Wood somewhere. There's an old castle where the fairies used to hide stolen babies, when it was still allowed.'

They flew over the tree tops searching for the castle. Suddenly Natasha spotted four turrets jutting just above the trees.

'That's it!' said Pillywiggins. 'And there's another clearing. Down. Now.'

Natasha tucked in her arms and descended rapidly.

Thwump. As she landed she sent up a cloud of ash. Ash! Oh no. But it was too late to change direction. When she opened her eyes she was staring into the cavernous mouth of a dragon. Teeth like stalagmites and stalactites lined the path to its throat. Red tonsils waggled at the back and its long tongue, slightly curled, was ready to scoop her down its throat.

Natasha recoiled at the heat, but couldn't move her feet.

Thinking her end had come, she closed her eyes and hoped it would all be over quickly. Silently she counted to ten to try and stop herself thinking about those sharp teeth.

Nothing.

Hearing a whimper, she opened her eyes warily and seemed to be looking up a bumpy green hill. The dragon's nose. Phew! He'd closed his mouth – almost – and he was going cross-eyed trying to see Pillywiggins who was standing between them. She'd lifted her invisibility spell.

The dragon's tongue was lashing from side to side, trying to catch her.

'Natasha, run!' she cried. 'Find the castle. I can deal with Hot Breath!'

Natasha ran.

She didn't know where. She just ran as fast as she could from the clearing, crashing through the undergrowth till she came to a sudden stop. There was something solid in front of her.

Was this the castle? She wondered as she saw her hands running over the bricks and tangled ivy. She could see her hands! Oh no! She was visible again she realised; the spell must have worn off.

Looking to her left she saw something

horrible. A Bugaboo, she was sure of it, guarding a door.

Huge, the Bugaboo's swinging arms nearly touched the ground. Skin like mouldy cheese hung from its body in folds. She couldn't see its face till it turned to look in her direction. Then she saw the single eye in the middle of its forehead.

Could it see her?

Natasha pressed herself to the wall and tried to keep her wits about her. But there was something else, a *smell* like stinky cheese which made her recoil even before she saw another, even bigger Bugaboo step out of the door.

Chapter 26

How could she get rid of them?

Looking round she spied a stone. Lowering herself to a crouching position, she picked it up. Then, copying an action of Jamie's, she skimmed it as far as she could deep into the wood.

Thank you, Jamie.

The creatures turned away from her. Did they think what she hoped they were thinking? Would they fall for her trick? She held her breath, trying to keep as still and quiet as she could.

The creatures grunted.

She threw another stone even further – and off they charged, ears flapping, arms swinging after some imagined foe.

Natasha almost leaped to the door but it was massive and the handle was at the top where only a Bugaboo could reach it.

'I wish—'

'I were here?'

'P-Pillywiggins!' Natasha gasped as she felt the fairy land on her shoulder. Pillywiggins was invisible again.

'I'll try to turn the handle,' said the fairy. 'When I say push, push as hard as you can.'

Natasha wanted to say, 'Couldn't you make me invisible first?' But felt Pillywiggins leave her shoulder.

'Push,' Pillywiggins gasped seconds later from above her.

Natasha threw her whole weight against the door and it opened.

'Come on,' whispered Pillywiggins, suddenly by her side again. 'We've got to find Green Baby.'

They were in a tall, narrow, windowless room, with doors at either end.

Dozens of babies lay in cots, two rows, one on either side of the room. The babies all looked the same, like human babies, only much paler, as if they'd never seen the light of day.

'The Fairy Queen will be shocked when I tell her about this,' said Pillywiggins. 'She has banned the ancient fairy game of stealing babies.'

'How will we know which one is Green Baby?' Natasha asked.

'I expect he'll look a bit like his mother,' said Pillywiggins.

None of them did, and Natasha couldn't help feeling a bit relieved. Did she want to meet something like Tree Witch? What if he behaved like her?

Then she reached the end of the row and saw a door opening.

Crouching behind a cot she saw a boy coming in. He looked a bit like a Christmas tree, she thought, without decorations.

Or like Tree Witch! Of course! Green Baby had grown! Natasha remembered what she had read about time being different in Fairy Land.

Suddenly Green Boy jumped forward as a long hairy brown arm reached out for him.

'Come back to the school room. You're a big

boy now.' The voice was whiny, as you'd expect from a creature whose voice came out of its nose.

'No, shan't!' Green Baby – or Green Boy – jumped out of the Brownie's reach.

'Come here!' The Brownie, who looked like a hairy ape, lumbered after Green Boy. But Green Boy had spotted the open door at the other end of the room and was heading for it.

The Brownie galumphed after him.

It was a race for the door.

'And Green Boy must win,' said Pilly-wiggins, suddenly overhead. 'Natasha, you distract the Brownie. I'll grab Green Boy.'

But they were too late. The Brownie had hold of Green Boy's hand.

Natasha couldn't see Pillywiggins but heard her voice saying, 'Let go of the boy, Brownie, I must take him to the Fairy Queen.'

But the Brownie didn't let go, and Natasha saw another one coming in through the door at the back. She had to do something – quick! What? She had an idea. But dare she? Yes! Springing from her hiding place she landed behind the Brownie, reached up and hoping it was ticklish, tickled it under its hairy arms. And it doubled up with laughter. And let go. It must have because suddenly Green Boy was flying through the door.

Natasha shot through after him – them – because Pillywiggins must be towing him.

'Close the door,' she heard the fairy gasp.

Natasha slammed it shut.

'The portal now,' said Pillywiggins. 'We're taking you home to your mother, Green Boy.'

But he wasn't listening. His face was scrunched up trying to keep out a horrible smell. So was Natasha's. So was Pillywiggins's.

The Bugaboos were back.

Chapter 27

Three Bugaboos were blocking their escape. No, *her* escape. As the Bugaboos started stomping towards her, ears flapping, Natasha realised she was alone.

Pillywiggins must have airlifted Green Boy to safety.

'Intruder. Intruder.' The Bugaboos chanted as they came closer.

Natasha thought her last moment had come. How would they do it? Press her to their mouldy bodies and squeeze? Suffocate her with their stink?

Just do it quickly, she thought as she closed her eyes.

Then there was a cry from above.

'Natasha! Hold out your arms! Open your eyes!'

Looking up she was dazzled. At first she couldn't see anything. Then she saw a swarm of sparkling creatures descending. Trooper fairies! As tiny hands tugged at her pyjamas she realised they were trying to get a grip. But with one hand only, because with the other they were all holding their noses. Even so some of them managed to sing as they lifted her into the sky:

'We will take you
We will take you
To our lovely Fairy Queen . . .'

'Oh no,' said Natasha, as she saw the castle below. All hope drained away as the fairies towed her towards the Fairy Queen. 'I'm doomed to stay here for ever.'

'No you're not,' said Pillywiggins's voice, close to her ear. 'You're safe now.'

'From Bugaboos maybe,' said Natasha. 'But how am I going to save Charlie and get Green Boy home if the Fairy Queen dubs me?'

'She won't,' said Pillywiggins. 'Trust me.'

She turned to the troopers. 'Fairies, you can let go of Natasha now, she can fly by herself. You must go back to the castle and rescue all the stolen babies and bring them to the palace!'

'Why?' complained one.

'Because the Fairy Queen said so,' said Pillywiggins. 'She's furious with you for causing all this mayhem. Stealing babies is not allowed anymore. You'd better hurry up. All the babies must be returned to their families.'

The fairies had been flying slowly, but now Natasha felt herself moving swiftly over the Dark Wood.

Pillywiggins, visible now, flew alongside Natasha. 'I wrote to the Queen explaining everything,' she said. 'How the fairies stole Green Baby from Tree Witch and how we've come here to rescue him.'

'So?' Natasha still didn't understand. 'Where are we going now?'

'To the Fairy Queen. She's trying to restore order by getting you and Green Boy back to Earth. The Red Goblins have got him.'

'What?' Natasha was shocked.

'It's OK,' said Pillywiggins. 'They're taking him to the portal, on the Fairy Queen's orders. He'll love the fast ride. Look down. There it is.'

All Natasha could see was the palace on top of the hill.

'The portal is at the bottom of the hill.' Pillywiggins pointed and Natasha saw the fairy ring.

The darker grass and white mushrooms showed up against the light grass. Now she remembered whirling down from Earth and landing on something. But there was nothing above the ring except blue sky, the sky she was in. 'I don't understand. How can Fairy Land have sky when it's under the Earth? And how do we get back to Earth?'

'Magic of course,' said Pillywiggins. 'It's all magic. Hold tight, we're descending now!'

Chapter 20

The Fairy Queen was standing just outside the circle. Green Boy was there too, with the Red Goblins. He waved cheerily when he saw Natasha but everyone else was silent.

'I've told him you're taking him home,' whispered Pillywiggins, 'if the Fairy Queen can cast a spell strong enough to undo all the bad magic.'

'Are you coming with us?' asked Natasha.

'It depends on the Fairy Queen,' murmured Pillywiggins. 'Look at her.'

With arms outstretched and eyes closed there was something about the Fairy Queen that reminded Natasha of Tree Witch. Power, that's what it was, the power of magic. It rippled through her. But was her magic strong enough to combat the evil unleashed by the fairies' bad deed? A deep hush fell over the company as the Fairy Queen began to speak.

'Descend, O Magic of the night
And give me power
A wrong to right.
For one day's eye, reverse our lore
Peace and order
To restore.'

No one moved as the sky darkened. Quite quickly day turned to night till the only light was a sliver of moon.

Then the Fairy Queen spoke again: 'Natasha and Pillywiggins, take Green Boy's hands and step inside the silver pool.'

The pool was in the middle of the fairy ring and when the three of them stood in it, the Fairy Queen raised her wand.

'Fairies, take your places in the ring,' she commanded. 'Then sing and dance widdershins!'

'Widdershins means backwards,' whispered Pillywiggins as the elf band started playing and the fairies began to dance round them singing.

'*You must leave us*
You must leave us
You must leave our Fairy Queen.
You must leave us
You must leave us
Go back to the earthly green.'

As the fairies danced faster and faster, Natasha caught glimpses of the Fairy Queen weaving spirals with her wand. Then — *whoosh!* — the three of them were flying as the pool erupted, flying on a whirling, swirling volcano of silver stars.

'We're off!' cried Pillywiggins.

'Where to?' gasped Green Boy.

'Home,' said Natasha, holding his hand tightly, but didn't add, 'I hope'.

Chapter 29

At first Natasha didn't realise she was home.

One moment she was flying with Green Boy and Pillywiggins. The next she was standing in a grassy circle at the bottom of a rocky ravine. Well that's what it looked like. She was wondering where she was when she felt herself growing – rapidly – and the huge rocks on either side of her started to look like armchairs and a sofa.

Natasha gasped for breath. It was such a relief to be back in the sitting room watching the grassy circle fade.

Tap tap. There was an anxious face at the window. Jamie's.

Remembering his warnings, she held out her hand in front of her. It was still there.

She looked down. So were her feet. So she was alive and she wasn't invisible.

'Ma!'

For a few seconds she'd forgotten about Green Boy, but now she felt his scratchy hand in hers.

'You want your mum? Of course. I'll take you back to her.' Natasha sounded more confident than she felt. She was scared of seeing Tree Witch. She would much rather have crept upstairs to bed. But Charlie's ride-on train by the door reminded her that she still had work to do. Scary work.

It was dark outside. Clouds covered the moon. She couldn't see any stars.

'Come on, Green Boy.' When she opened the back door, there was Jamie staring at her.

'Are you OK?' He looked stunned. 'You didn't do what I said.'

'I'm fine. Meet Green Boy. I'm taking him back to his mother. Green Lady,' she added. 'Please, Jamie, stop staring.'

It was good to have Jamie by her side, but she turned down his offer to go with her to the garden. She had to do this alone. Tree Witch had said so. She didn't want to risk angering her. So Jamie held back the loose slat while she and Green Boy climbed through the fence. It was only when she passed where the statue had stood – there was only a mushroom there now – that she remembered Pillywiggins.

Where was she?

It was very quiet in the garden. Hardly a leaf stirred as she led Green Boy towards Tree Witch. Green Lady, she told herself. Natasha was sure she was watching, though it was too dark to see her. She felt her waiting. Then the moon came out from behind a cloud, creating a pool of light, and there she was, the witch. Definitely still a witch. Huge and spiky, she loomed over them. And then she saw them. Natasha knew the moment it happened.

Suddenly Tree Witch started shaking. Natasha felt the tremor, or was it her own shaking? She was terrified. The witch looked huge and sounded angry.

Natasha tried to say, 'H-here's your son,' but no words came out. She just stood there, hoping Tree Witch could see him.

Then it started to rain.

Plip. Plip. Plip.

Cold drops soaked into her pyjamas, but she couldn't move. She heard a sob and suddenly realised it wasn't rain falling. Looking up, she saw the drops were tears, Tree Witch's tears. Tree Witch was weeping. Tears were falling from her eyes as she leaned forward and held out her arms.

'Go to your mum, Green Boy.' Natasha pushed him gently forward.

He ran towards her and the tree's colour softened. Her shape softened. No longer stiff and spiky she leaned over, put out her arms and enfolded her son.

'Come on.' Jamie was by Natasha's side. 'Your job is done.'

But Natasha waited a few moments more, till she was sure that Tree Witch was transformed. Till Green Lady stood before her, tall and beautiful with Green Boy in her arms.

Charlie was fast asleep when Natasha crept into his room. He murmured when she picked up his hand but didn't wake up. She held his fingers in the glow of his night-light and saw

that his nails, all his nails, were pink. Filled with joy she went to bed. Glancing at her bedside clock she noticed the time. Five minutes past midnight. But it couldn't be. She'd been gone for hours, a whole day at least. That's what it seemed like.

And that's what it felt like the next morning when she woke up and remembered everything that had happened. Another good thing, she hadn't lost her memory. The Fairy Queen's magic spell had worked. She hadn't changed at all, she thought, till she went downstairs for breakfast.

When she walked into the kitchen the whole family was round the table.

Dad was telling Jonathan to hurry up with the cereal. Mum was telling Charlie to use a spoon. It was an ordinary morning. Then suddenly they were all staring at her.

'Gosh, Natasha,' said her dad. 'You've grown in the night. People say it sometimes happens.'

Her mum said, 'You do look bigger and older. Jonathan, stand back to back with Natasha.'

Jonathan didn't want to, but he stood up

grumpily, and was even grumpier when Natasha proved to be taller than him by about a centimetre. She had grown!

Worried that she might still be growing, she hurried upstairs to the long mirror in her bedroom.

Yes, she looked a bit older and – she stood against her measuring chart – she was fifteen centimetres taller than the last time she'd measured herself. When was that? She couldn't remember.

After breakfast she measured herself again and she was still the same height. Good. She didn't want to go on growing. She didn't want to be a giant. Fifteen centimetres would do nicely – for a bit. Fifteen centimetres would give the other girls quite a surprise. Titch she wasn't. She set off for school eagerly by the short cut.

The garden was peaceful. Bees buzzed. Grasses stirred. Green Lady looked lovely and Green Boy was bouncing gently at the end of one of her long branches. It was the branch where the rabbit used to sit, Natasha realised even before it hopped in front of her – a real live rabbit which looked up at her and wiffled its nose.

'He's saying thank you,' said a voice. 'And so am I.' It was Pillywiggins. 'I hid while you took Green Boy back to his mother, but I think it's safe to show myself now.'

Natasha looked up. The tree was a tree again, tall and beautiful, and yes, she thought, happy.

'I'm free to come and go now,' said Pillywiggins, 'here and in Fairy Land.'

'Well, I hope you'll visit the garden from time to time,' said another voice.

'Jamie!' Natasha gave him a hug.

'All's well that ends well,' said Pillywiggins, fluttering over their heads.

THE TIME-TRAVELLING CAT

Topher has a remarkable cat. She can travel through time but she always has trouble getting home! So poor Topher finds himself visiting Aztec warriors, Ancient Egyptian temples and Elizabethan magicians in order to rescue her!

'Intriguing and well-written' *Books for Keeps*

ISBN: 9781842706176

ISBN: 9781842706862

ISBN: 9781849390194

ISBN: 9781842705162

ISBN: 9781842705216

ISBN: 9781842706169

All £4.99

AUNT SEVERE and the DRAGONS

by Nick Garlick
Illustrations by Nick Maland

When Daniel's explorer parents vanish, he has to live with his strict and rather strange Aunt Severe.

But just when everything seems to be going wrong for Daniel, he meets four dragons hiding in the garden. They tell him about their lost magic book, The Spelldocious. But as soon as they leave the garden three of the dragons are captured by evil Gotcha Grabber, who throws them into his zoo.

With the help of Dud, a rather clumsy dragon, Daniel must try to rescue them and find the missing Spelldocious.

Nick Maland won the Booktrust Early Years Award and was shortlisted for Mother Goose Best Newcomer.

9781849390552 £4.99

Ms Wiz

by **TERENCE BLACKER**
with illustrations by **Tony Ross**

Ms Wiz always comes when Magic is needed, and Class Five do test that in every way. After all, a paranormal operative is a handy person to have helping out – whether it's arranging class trips to tropical islands, or finding a lost cat.

'Funny, magical . . . with wicked pictures by Tony Ross, it's the closest thing you'll get to Roald Dahl.'
The Times

All £4.99

ISBN: 9781842707029

ISBN: 9781842707036

ISBN: 9781842708477

ISBN: 9781842708484

ISBN: 9781842708583

DAMIAN DROOTH SUPERSLEUTH

ACE DETECTIVE

by Barbara Mitchelhill

with illustrations by
Tony Ross

Damian Drooth is a super sleuth, a number
one detective, a kid with a nose for trouble.
And here in this fantastic bumper edition are
three of his hilarious stories:
*The Case of the
Disappearing Daughter,
How to Be a Detective*
and *The Case of the
Popstar's Wedding.*

'Madcap cartoon-
sketch humour'
TES

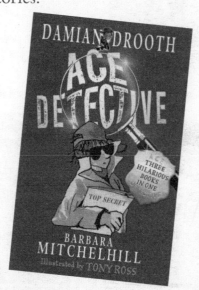

9781849390972 £5.99